Growing Smarter

Written by Judith V.T. Wilson

Pictures by Christopher Saghy

Printed in the United States of America

ISBN-13: 9780991244287
ISBN-10: 0991244281

Cover and Interior art by Christopher Saghy

MAPLE CREEK MEDIA

MAPLE CREEK MEDIA

P.O. Box 624
Hampstead, MD 21074
Toll-Free Phone: 1-877-866-8820
Toll-Free Fax: 1-877-778-3756
Email: info@maplecreekmedia.com
Website: www.maplecreekmedia.com

This book is dedicated to my husband, who has not only supported my endeavors but also has endured my long hours devoted to school work, and to my son, who spent many extra hours in my classroom during his elementary school years. ~ Judy

For Kathy, Shannon and Michael... and for everyone who has ever struggled with learning something new and kept at it until they got it right. Never give up! ~ Christopher

About this book...

This book was written to inform educators as well as parents about how young brains can get smarter. The research behind a growth mindset explains how adopting this belief can impact a child's education, career, and life. Although its story is an easy-read, its message is a powerful one that can be read over and over to empower all children as they grow up and learn new things. Parents will find themselves repeating Mama and Papa Owl's words in their children's own real life situations. Those same words will echo throughout children's lives as parents adlib key messages to foster a growth mindset in the future. Plus, educators can utilize this story as a read-aloud to open conversations about a growth mindset and reference it frequently throughout the year as challenges are faced in the classroom. Because all teachers hold high expectations for their students, this book will undoubtedly become a favorite staple vital to promoting a growth mindset for all students in the 21st century classroom.

I am just a little owl now, but I will grow up to be a big owl someday.
I will grow up to be a big owl like Mama Owl and Papa Owl.

Mama Owl says I must **eat good food** to grow up **to be big and strong!**

My **beak** will grow **bigger...**

and my **talons** will grow **sharper.**

My **wings** will grow much larger and longer **for flying.**

Papa Owl will teach me how to fly.

I know learning to fly will not be easy for me, but he says I must not be scared. Even when I am sitting high in a tall, tall tree, I must not be scared to fly.

Grandma Owl says I cannot be afraid of failing on my first try. In fact, Papa Owl says it is okay to fail, because I am learning something new. They both know flying is hard to do for a little owl. Mama Owl even says that **making mistakes is part of learning.** She tells me not to give up. I must stick with it until I can fly like big owls do.

I must keep trying harder and harder to fly a little higher each time. I have to try again... even when I fall to the ground.

Here I go...

Oh, no!

Not again!

Why can't I fly?

Papa Owl tells me it looks like I have a problem with flying. What can I do to help me fly? **I have to solve my problem.**

Hmmm… Let me think. I want to do a little better. I want to fly a little higher in the sky. So I think **I will take off my wet sweater** and stretch my wings out more.

I can do it!

I am able to fly over the trees. I can fly as high as Mama Owl and Papa Owl now. And Papa Owl tells me I am a good problem solver, too.

I feel so proud of myself!

I feel good about not giving up. I know now that trying hard was worth it. I even solved a problem on my own too.

Now that I am able to fly, I am big enough to go to school like Mama Owl and Papa Owl did when they were growing up. **Papa Owl tells me that I have to grow up to be a wise old owl.** Grandpa Owl is very wise. Grandma Owl is very wise, too. Mama Owl says I will have to go to school to learn.

Mama Owl says I will get smart at school. I know I was born with a brain and I want to get smart. I want to get smarter and smarter so I can grow up to become a wise old owl.

Papa Owl and Mama Owl tell me that my brain will grow strong -- just like my wings did when I was learning to fly. They tell me that my brain is like a muscle and it can grow smarter. **I did not know that!**

Grandpa Owl tells me I can get smarter and smarter every year. Even though I am a little owl now, I can get smarter as I grow up. He says my brain is small now because I am young. But since my brain will grow as I grow, **I must train my brain.**

Papa Owl is a wise old owl, and he says the same thing Grandpa Owl does about my brain. I must remember that **my brain is like a muscle that can get stronger and smarter.** I must remember how I used the muscles in my wings when I flew high into the sky and how my wing muscles got stronger and stronger so I could fly higher and higher.

So now I need to exercise my brain when I am at school because it is like a muscle, too. My brain will grow stronger and I will grow smarter every time I learn something new.

At school, I will learn to read and write. I will also learn to do math. All of those things are new to me now as a little owl. Everything will be new to learn like when I was trying to learn to fly for the first time. But I will take on that challenge. **I will put my mind to it.**

Mama Owl says I must have a strong mindset and push myself. I know my brain can get smarter when I am learning. **So I will make up my mind to do it.**

I am not afraid to make mistakes at school now, because **I know I can learn from my mistakes.** Papa Owl wants me to try hard. He lets me make mistakes because he knows I will be learning something new as my brain is learning.

When I put my mind and effort into what I do, my brain gets stronger and smarter. Papa Owl likes when I stick with doing things that are hard for me to do.

At school I will learn more than just how to do math or read books.
I will learn how to be a thinker. I will learn to stretch my thinking
like I stretched my wings to fly high. Mama Owl wants me to think and
think and think. Mama Owl says my brain is making new connections
inside my head which are making me smarter. She is a wise old owl, too.

Grandpa Owl wants me to think about everything. He wants me to think hard, too. Grandpa Owl is always asking me, **"What do you think?"**

I like thinking out loud, too. Papa Owl even asks me, "What do you think would happen if ...?" That is a challenge question for me, but it is a game we like to play to exercise my brain.

I like stretching my thinking, too. I like thinking about a lot of different things. I like to think about math, science, and social studies. I sometimes think about why trees lose their leaves in Autumn, why fish swim upstream, and why owls say, **"Hoot-Hoo!"**

Mama Owl tells me that school will get more challenging as I get older. But I believe **my brain has room to grow** and will get smarter.

Papa Owl knows that **there is always something to be learned** even when I make mistakes or do not succeed the first time.

I feel smart knowing that my brain will grow.

I can push myself to learn anything now. I can tell myself that I may not be able to do it yet, but I will be able to do it later if I put my mind to it. I have brain power and the mindset to succeed.

And so do you!

About The Author:

Judy Wilson has enjoyed a long and accomplished career in education. Her first twenty years were spent as a classroom teacher at both elementary and secondary levels. She later transitioned into staff development where keeping abreast of current trends in education has been energizing and rewarding. She is a national board certified teacher and earned a Masters of Science in Curriculum and Instruction in addition to an Administrator 1 certification. Her talent has always been to transform theory and research into practical applications in the classroom. She has designed and implemented many innovative learning experiences that ultimately led to her being named **Teacher of the Year** in her school district. Her many local and state awards have stemmed from her creative ability to make real life connections across the curriculum into experiences that engage and motivate all students.

Judy grew up in West Virginia with her ponies practically in the backyard. She taught in several school systems in West Virginia and Maryland. Judy lives in Delaware with her husband and rescued cat. She enjoys relaxing outside on her deck, picking crabs, growing herbs, and listening to the owls in the nearby woods.

- -

About The Illustrator/Designer:

Designer and Illustrator Christopher Saghy spends the better part of his life in his studio drawing, painting, coloring and/or creating digital art while listening to everything from old radio shows to Frank Sinatra to B.B. King to Jimi Hendrix to Holst. ("Each project seems to have it's own unique soundtrack.") He creates because he is compelled to do so… often stating that he "could give up breathing only slightly easier than drawing."

Christopher has numerous book cover designs and/or illustrations to his credit as well as having written and illustrated *"The Easy-to-Read, RHYMING, With-Really-Cool-Pictures ABC Book."* (Available directly from Old Line Publishing, Amazon.com or Barnes & Noble.com.)

For *"Growing Smarter,"* Christopher designed all the characters, rendered the illustrations -- a mix of traditional and digital art -- as well as handling the layout, typography and graphic design for the entire book.

Visit him on Facebook at Christopher Saghy - Illustration and Design.

CPSIA information can be obtained
at www.ICGtesting.com
Printed in the USA
BVOW05*2012030317

477707BV00009B/23/P